DATE DUE	
JAN 6 – 2005	
FEB 1 7 2007	
MAR 2 6 2007	

DEMCO, INC. 38-2931

Henry's Amazing Machine

— ☆ —

Dayle Ann Dodds

Pictures by Kyrsten Brooker

Melanie Kroupa Books
Farrar, Straus and Giroux • New York

*For Greg, who knows how to put things together
better than* anyone—*except Henry, of course!*
—D.D.

For John, with love always
—K.B.

Text copyright © 2004 by Dayle Ann Dodds
Illustrations copyright © 2004 by Kyrsten Brooker
All rights reserved
Distributed in Canada by Douglas & McIntyre Ltd.
Color separations by Hong Kong Scanner Arts
Printed and bound in the United States of America by Berryville Graphics
Designed by Jennifer Browne
First edition, 2004
1   3   5   7   9   10   8   6   4   2

www.fsgkidsbooks.com

Library of Congress Cataloging-in-Publication Data
Dodds, Dayle Ann.
    Henry's amazing machine / by Dayle Ann Dodds ; pictures by Kyrsten Brooker.— 1st ed.
        p. cm.
    Summary: Henry finally finds a purpose for the "Incredible, Amazing Machine" that he built.
    ISBN 0-374-32953-2
    [1. Machinery—Fiction.   2. Inventors—Fiction.]   I. Brooker, Kyrsten, ill.   II. Title.

PZ7.D66285 He 2004
[E]—dc21

                                                                                            2002029783

From the time Henry was a baby, he loved putting things together.

He put wheels with rods.
He put switches with levers.
He put cranks with gears in the most unusual ways.

He made his parents proud.

By the age of six, Henry had built an Amazing Machine. It filled his entire room. But Henry didn't mind. He moved into the bathroom and kept on building.

By eight, Henry's machine filled the living room, the dining room, and the hallway.

But Henry didn't mind. He moved into the kitchen, and kept on building . . .

and building . . .

and BUILDING.

Henry's parents were still proud, but they were beginning to worry.

"Now, Henry," they said. "You have

"Whirling things, twirling things,
Zipping, zapping, swirling things,
Clunking things, thunking things,
Slipping, sliding, dunking things!

"You sure know how to build things, but, Henry, what
does it DO?"

"DO?" said Henry. "I haven't a clue."

And Henry just smiled and kept on building.

By the time Henry was ten, his Amazing Machine had taken up so much of the house that his family had to move out into the backyard and pitch a tent. But that didn't stop Henry.

When he had finished building INSIDE,
he moved OUTSIDE.

Into the front yard . . .

Then the side yard . . .

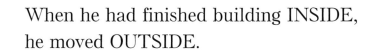

But when he rounded the corner and headed for the backyard, Henry's father said, "Now, Henry. You have

"Dripping things, dropping things,
Pushing, pulling, stopping things,
Clanking things, cranking things,
Stretching, bending, spanking things!"

And Henry's mother said, "Now, Henry. You have

"Whipping things, whapping things,
Clapping, snapping, slapping things,
Tracking things, hacking things,
Smacking, cracking, whacking things!

"You sure know how to build things,
BUT, HENRY, WHAT DOES IT DO?"

"Do?" said Henry. "I haven't a clue."

And Henry just smiled and kept on building.

Henry's Incredible, Amazing Machine took over every inch of the yard. It grew so big, in fact, that Henry's parents were forced to move out of their tent and up into the giant oak tree.

Soon people came from far and wide to see what Henry had built.

Little Jeremy put up a stand and sold
cups of ice-cold lemonade for twenty-five cents.

Grandpa Jack and Old Charley put aside their
quarreling and set up their checkerboard nearby to
watch the goings-on.

The Widow Hiccup, who had not been seen for years,
creaked open her dusty front door and ventured out
on the porch to see what all the hubbub was about.

Wussmeyer's House of Wieners served
plump, juicy franks hot off the grill.

Mrs. Rose, the church organist, got into the act.
She had her organ rolled to Henry's house, and she
played all sorts of lively tunes to add to the fun.

Even Mr. Barnaby showed up with his
tired old carnival pony to give children
rides in front of Henry's machine.

Before long, the High School Marching Band arrived, followed by the Gymnastics Club and the Tri-City Tappers, who flipped and twirled, tapped and swirled.

People sang, people danced, people ate, and people talked until the wee hours of the morning.

Henry's parents were still very proud, but they were getting a little tired of living up in the tree house. There was no heat and little space, and worst of all, in order to collect their mail, they had to catch the paper airplanes the mailman made out of their letters.

What's more, with all the noise outside, Henry's parents could hardly catch a wink of sleep.

Finally, they pulled Henry aside and said, "Now, Henry. You have

"Bumping things, thumping things,
Mixing, pouring, dumping things,
Bubbling things, doubling things,
Spinning, shooting, troubling things!

"Enough is enough. Your machine has to go."

Sadly, the next morning, Henry stopped building, turned off his machine, and put up a sign:

An INCREDIBLE, AMAZING Machine
Free to a good home.

Soon the lemonade stand closed up shop. Grandpa Jack and Old Charley folded their checkerboard. The hot dog grill cooled off, the organ was rolled back to the church, and the Widow Hiccup disappeared inside her house once more.

Even Mr. Barnaby led his tired old carnival pony away.

There was nothing more for Henry to build. He walked and walked until the moon rose up in the sky.

There, at the end of the road, he met Mr. Barnaby, hammering a CLOSED sign on the carnival gate.

"Goodbye, Henry," Mr. Barnaby said. "My pony and I are leaving town. No one comes to my little carnival anymore. I don't know what else to do."

"DO?" said Henry. "*Now* I have a clue!"

The next day the mailman was busy delivering special invitations to everyone in town.

Dressed in their best, Grandpa Jack, Old Charley, little Jeremy, the Widow Hiccup, Mrs. Rose, Mr. Wussmeyer, and the others paraded down the road, led by the High School Marching Band, the Gymnastics Club, and, of course, the Tri-City Tappers.

When they reached the carnival gate, they couldn't believe their eyes.

Mr. Barnaby
and
Henry
request your company at
the Grand Opening of the
B & H CARNIVAL
Tomorrow 2:00 p.m.

Hiccup
Lane

There were

Whipping things, whapping things,
Whirling, twirling, zapping things,
Clunking things, thunking things,
Slipping, sliding, dunking things,
Dripping things, dropping things,
Pushing, pulling, stopping things,
Clanking things, cranking things,
Stretching, bending, spanking things,
Bumping things, thumping things,
Mixing, pouring, dumping things!

"You sure know how to build things!" little Jeremy
exclaimed. Everyone cheered.

"THANK YOU, HENRY!"

"HENRY?"